# Bed Head

## Written by Nancy Bennetts

### Illustrated by Lance Bowen

### Creative design & Layout by Ed. Kesterson

## Published by:

Kesterson & Associates
516 North Chinowth
Visalia, CA 93291

## Illustrations:

Lance Bowen, Geezer Graphics

## Design and Layout:

Ed. Kesterson, Kesterson & Associates

ISBN: 0-9726004-1-8

Printed in Hong Kong

1st Printing

**Dedicated to
Children everywhere.
May your lives be filled
with love, peace
and the sounds of laughter.**

*"I praise you because
I am fearfully and wonderfully made."*

**Psalm 139: 14a NIV**

*"And even the very hairs of your head
are all numbered."*

**Matthew 10: 30 NIV**

**Have you ever wondered what happens at night,**

**After you've gone to bed and turned out the lights?**

After you've had your bath and brushed your teeth?

After you've been read a story and tucked gently into bed to sleep?

I wonder!
What makes you
wake up and get
such a fright,

When you look in
the mirror and see
what happened
last night?

**Did the fairies come out and dance on your head?**

# Did you stand on your head and twist left and right?

Did the dog lick
your hair?

*Did your cat make a nest?*

What made you wake up with a bad case of bed head?

There is
blond hair
bed head.

There is
brown hair
bed head.

There is really
wild-red hair
bed head.

*Is there black hair bed head?*

# Yep!

There is
thin hair bed head.

There is
thick hair
bed head.

There is curly hair bed head, and there is straight hair bed head.

There is no
no-hair
bed head.

**No!**
**Not that kind of hare**
**bed head.**

Maybe, you should
have someone
stay up in the night.

Have them
sit in a chair
and keep watch
on your hair.

**Then, when you wake up,
you will know why
your hair stands on end
and sticks out
left and right.**

It makes no difference
if your hair
is blond, brown, red or black.

**When you look in the mirror and see yourself looking back...**

**with your hair all tousled, snaggled, and snarled...**

You can smile,
laugh, and giggle too...
for in the morning
your friends look
just like you.

# The End!